MORE OF

CAPTAIN WORTHY'S
WARSHIP ADVENTURES

WILLIAM MILBORN

authorHOUSE®

AuthorHouse™
1663 Liberty Drive
Bloomington, IN 47403
www.authorhouse.com
Phone: 1 (800) 839-8640

Published by AuthorHouse 03/19/2019

ISBN: 978-1-7283-0483-0 (sc)
ISBN: 978-1-7283-0482-3 (e)

SYNOPSIS FOR SEQUEL

This sequel begins exactly where the story stops in the first book. It's just like turning the last page of the first book to the first page of the sequel.

Commander Worthy finds that his visit to his brother-in-law revealed a tragedy and threatening of his brother-in-law's family. You will see how that crisis is resolved by a good commander and his young son, Will. Captain Worthy and his accompanying Captain John's Warship, was now responsible for moving a strange cargo back to Cuba. There the captain and his escort ships encountered three life-and-death events that occurred on the high seas. You will find that the resolution of these crisis' will be very interesting and frightening.

On return to Cuba, the captain discovers he is about to be confronted with an armada of Spanish ships that are directed to take back to Cuba which that call "Little Spain".

You will follow him through the planning of and taking part in the biggest warship battle of his career. Late in this action-packed book Captain Worthy's major decision is to carry him to a new adventure. You will get to know several fascinating characters, one who is called Booker T. T. Master, better known to all that knew him as the "Tall Thin Man" (for T. T.).

This is an action-packed book with the real possibility of there needing to be another sequel to cover the new adventures of Captain Worthy, his friends, and his family.

There are so many new adventures to be told, I cannot mention them all in this sequel. Truthfully, I have yet to get them all on paper.

ACKNOWLEDGEMENTS

Author:	William L. Milborn
Artwork, editing, typing:	Terri L. Milborn
Final editing and Computer entry:	Carolyn A. Fischer

There has been a lot that has happened since the revelations I described in my last Warship Adventures. First, as many of my readers know, as you become older you become a bit smarter in many ways. My wife Annabelle and I both agree that I should try to avoid personal confrontations such as duels with assorted weapons. We agree I am far more vulnerable at this point in my life than I was years ago. I now try to avoid situations where some younger person thinks he needs to achieve fame by challenging me to a duel. I used to think mostly of taking such a person to task. Now, I avoid situations that arise to cause a life-or-death duel simply to give satisfaction to either my opponent or myself.

How? When challenged, I now give the challenger the opportunity to "save face" by letting him win the challenge he's given and say, "Whatever will please you, but fighting a duel until one of us dies is not the answer to your feelings you have toward me or my cause. Therefore, I agree that whatever your complaint is, I acknowledge it and give in to your request, and we will both live to enjoy another day." You must understand, however, there are certain limits to this matter of fighting. I certainly am capable of fighting during sea battles or on land as well, when it is a matter of life-or-death.

As you remember in the previous adventure, I had taken my son, Will, back to Ireland to replenish the Irish Whiskey needed to supply our casino in Cuba and visit Annabelle's brother in England. Remember Aaron insisted that he stay in England to continue the operations of the pub called the Bounty and that he had a family and horse farm and did not want to move.

I am anguished to report that Aaron, my beloved brother-in-law, had lost everything. When we docked my ship the Annabelle, with my support ship, we went directly to Aaron's home where I found him losing himself in a tankard of rum. He looked at me and with tears in his eyes said, "Thank God you're here! My wife, children, and I do not know what to do since our pub the Bounty is now burned to ashes. I must somehow find a way to support my wife and our two children. What will I do with all those wonderful singers and dancers that had a job at the Bounty? They too are wondering what they should do."

I said, "Aaron, I have the means to immediately remove all your worries that you have for your family and friends. This is what I offer to do for you and those you care for. I will spend several days with you, sell your horse farm, your home and belongings, except for those items you and your wife wish to keep. We will then move you, your family and friends to Cuba where I will provide you with a home and a job for you at the Cuban casino. Annabelle would love to have you help her manage the casino the same way you did with the Bounty pub. You would manage the bar and whiskey and sales. Annabelle will continue to manage the entertainment. We will get your children enrolled in the Havana school."

Aaron looked into my eyes and said, "May I call you Joseph when others aren't around?" I said, "Yes you may. Why do you ask?" Aaron replied, "I have something terrible to say---I may have been the cause for the Bounty burning and the threat of death to my family." I could see that Aaron was so distraught that he could hardly say the words he next told me. Between sobs, Aaron said, "I had a claims race between my best horse and a thoroughbred horse from the Royal Stables. I won his very best horse that he put up against mine. His horse was his major breeding horse and winner of many races at Epson Downs.

He protested the outcome. At the end of that race he challenged the outcome and that my horse did not win by a nose. Nevertheless, the officials handed me the reins of his thoroughbred and said it was mine. His horse was named Royal Best and the owners name was Edward Heathman."

"I took advantage of your name and called by best horse Trustworthy. Heathman threatened me by saying, return my thoroughbred 'Royal Best' to me and your nag 'Trustworthy', or you will regret it." The next day he sent his colleague to tell me he would burn down my pub and kill a member of my family by Friday of this week if I did not comply. He pushed me to comply with his demands.

"Joseph, what should I do?" He had kept his threat so far and burned down the pub and now I fear for my family. There was a long pause before I said to Aaron, "My God, Aaron, you have no choice but to submit to his commands. You must meet him at your horse barn for the transfer of ownership of "Trustworthy" and return his horse "Royal Best" to him. I told Heathman that I would bring my brother-in-law and he must bring a representative. I stayed with Aaron and his family that night.

It was mid-day when we met his representative and said they would meet with Aaron and present the transfer of ownership of "Royal Best" on Thursday at my stable. Aaron Said, "My horses and racing them is the best thing I had in life besides my family and that to give them up would be very hard, but it's the only choice I have rather than risk my family from the threats of the powerful owner Heathman."

Finally, it was the next day, when Edward Heathman and his colleague met with us in front of the stables. Heathman stuck out his hand and said, "Good choice, Aaron O'Hara! You agree no words will be said to anyone about this arrangement or I will hurt your family." Aaron brought his horse, "Trustworthy", out to the barn and tied it to the post next to Heathman's thoroughbred. Aaron and I did not offer to shake hands with Heathman. He said, "Don't anger me!" Apparently Heathman was unimpressed that I, Captain Joseph Worthy, was dressed as a Captain Commander with epee at my side. It was far beyond Heathman's belief that anyone could be a threat to him.

At that point I stepped forward and faced Heathman. I said, "Sir, this is not over. You have been threatening Aaron and his family with death and cheated him out of his horse which he rightfully won. Now place your weapon on the ground for one of us will die this mid-day!" Heathman did not respond, instead he placed his hand on his pistol.

"You and your thugs burned down Aaron O'Hara's means of a living. Now you have taken his horse he won, and his own horse and threatened death to his family. Trust me…you will not live through this!!!" I looked at Aaron and said, "Killing him is the best I can do for you! Is this what you want?"

Aaron quickly responded, "No, I will not put your life in jeopardy for my problems, I would rather you not kill a man, though I know you easily could! Is there another way Captain Joseph?" I looked at Heathman and saw the evidence of his fear by just looking at his wet pants. He had wetted himself clear through his pants at just the thought of a duel.

I said, "You do not have to die by a duel. I am going tpo let both of you sit down by the barn door and let you think about it while I talk to my brother-in-law. I'll just take your pistol so you won't be tempted to have a surprise duel." Aaron and I stepped to where the horses were standing, which was about fifteen yards from where Heathman was sitting. I said, "Aaron, there are three ways to go. The first way is to kill Heathman and send his colleague back to London with a true story of Heathman's burning your pub and threatening your family with death, all for the sake of two horses. The second option is to keep the horses and let them go free after we set sail. Finally, I love the third option best of all---Take these rascals with us and let them travel with us to Cuba.

Maybe Aaron, after setting up your horse stable in Cuba, you could let Heathman and his colleague be your stable boy and groom! Aaron, taking the life of a coward who cannot defend himself is against my code of ethics. You are going to keep your horses and I will buy a merchant ship that can handle animals. We are going to load the best twelve of your horses for their transport along with enough hay, grain and water to feed them on their journey. Aaron, do you like this plan?" "Yes, I do", he replied, "But what do we do with these two until everything for the ship can be bought and the horses be put on board and all of my belongings stored on the ship?"

"No Aaron, you have it wrong. You, your family and your belongings will be on that merchant ship. I will escort you to Cuba. Don't worry Aaron, I will use or resell that merchant ship when I get to Cuba. I will keep Heathman and his cohort in my brig aboard the Annabelle. How does that sound?" "Great!", he replied. I said, "Now Aaron, as a Master and Commander of a fleet I must always look ahead for treachery, theft and other problems. I have applied this knowledge after you told me the story of how this all came about. I will have what I call my warrior seamen circumvent your property and approach your land as your enemies and Heathman's evil companions might do." Lo-and-behold, we found them just beyond the O'Hara's bridge! There were six of them that had been hired by Heathman. They would back up his demands. "Did you, just a minute ago, hear three shots fired west of your land? That was a signal that we found them." I walked to Heathman and his colleague and said, "I may not kill you. I have a different plan for you, but until then one of you will be locked in the tool shed and the other in the barn. His colleague was a pudgy little fat man who apparently could not speak.

One of my warrior seamen said, "Here those devils come, tied to each other and let by my crewmen." I said to my warrior leader Mr. Raven, "Place those devil scoundrels into that small corral."

I said, "Now one of you who are Heathman's henchmen, will be dealt with differently. You will face a different fate." One of my warrior crewmen said, "Sir, can we keep the tall, thin man? He had no weapons and quoted Shakespeare." I said, "Thank you seaman, bring him to me---I would like to speak to him." I asked Thinman, "Why were you with these henchmen?" Thinman replied, "Heathman paid me to teach him about numbers, reading and writing." I said, "Mr. Thinman just briefly tell me what your skills are." He said, "Captain Sir, I can speak fluent Spanish, German, French and Italian. I can also write in those languages. I speak a little of the Danish language and Gaelic language. I am a chef trained in France and I am especially skilled in the epee and the pistol, which I learned via the courtesy of a master swordsman." I was totally astonished. I said, "Everyone, listen to me. Mr. Thinman will become our teacher in the basic skills of writing, reading and numbers, as well as languages. But first Mr. Thinman, speak to me in each of those languages. What is your name? What is your cargo? Where are you bound? How many men do you have? Now go ahead, there are enough men here to recognize if you are speaking the language of their country. Go ahead and do so." Mr. Thinman did exactly that. He not only spoke the languages, but he could say them like Shakespeare might. I said, "Outstanding Thinman! You had tweaked my interest when you said you knew the epee and are a master at using it. I am considered the best around. I want you to teach me the skill as you know it to be as taught by a French Master." I said, "Aaron, put a cork on each of our blades. We do not necessarily want to spill blood during this first teaching assignment." The Thinman took a position as a Master Swordsman would. With his arm over his head, he cut circles in the air with his epee signifying that he was ready to fight.

For some reason I chuckled at the thought that this very tall, thin man who was also very scrawny, could teach me a skill with the epee. It is embarrassing to tell you this man thwarted every epee strike to his body whether my epee struck upwards, downwards or sideways.

In fact, I attempted straightforward lunges to all parts of his body and never once did I touch him. "Let us put an end to this, Sir." With a twirl of his epee to my epee, he flipped the epee right out of my hand. Besides he caught my epee by the handle on its way downward. It was like magic and then he said, "I would be happy to teach that move and others too, if you desired, but never ask me to kill with it."

I know my face was red and I felt embarrassment in front of my crewmen. I said, "You mentioned that you were a good shot Mr. Thin Man. Take this sidearm which is ready to shoot and see how close you can come with a musket ball to the center of that pail sitting by the well, which I estimate to be thirty meters from where we stand." Thin Man immediately raised his arm and placed the barrel of the pistol upon his forearm and without hesitation aimed and shot.

The bucket stood in place but rocked to-and-fro. He hit it dead center, and the bucket spewed the water contained in it. Now shoot the beehive in that tree just to the left of the well. He looked at me and said, "Sir, would that not be a bit unfair to the bees since they have not harmed us?"

"Mr. Thin Man", I said, "I am amazed at your skills." I continued, "I have not decided where you would be of most usefulness to our company. I do not want you to teach skills in firearms to anyone except me. I want you to be clear on that demand. I am going to build you a school house where you can teach reading, writing and the numbers. I want everyone in your classes which includes my officers, to learn the skills of reading, writing and the numbers. You may teach languages only to my officers and myself. I would like you to teach all three skills to myself in my private quarters. And also teach me the skills you possess for the epee and the pistol."

Mr. Thin Man said, "Captain, Sir, you have given me a new life. I cannot thank you enough. I do have one small request that in speaking about teaching numbers, it is now called mathematics---reading, writing and mathematics!"

I said, "Consider it done, Mr. Thin Man. I am going to register your new existence under a new name. You are to be known as Mr. Booker T. T. Masters. The T. T. is for tall, thin. You will be referred to as Mr. Booker or Mr. Masters, whichever you prefer. It seems appropriate since you will be the school master of your school. I wish for you to find men and women who have some knowledge of these skills and teach them more and let them help you teach the many students which I am sure you will have."

Mr. Masters said, "Captain Sir, I have teaching books in my saddlebags that contain language and mathematics lessons. If you could print copies of these books, I could use them when teaching your officers languages. Everyone could read and study them as well."

I said, "Lieutenant, spread the word to all ships that Mr. Booker T. T. Masters will be among us. His rank as Master will be considered the same as Captain and he will receive Captain's pay. Lieutenant, take Mr. Booker T. T. Masters and put him in a fine cabin on my ship. When we arrive in Cuba, I will buy him a two-person carriage and bring one of my brother-in-law's finest horses, just like the dignitaries have. Since you were a groomsman, you will know how to care for and stable this fine horse."

"You will be taken to the clothier where you will receive three fine suits that are suitable for a teacher. That is all. I thank you Mr. Booker T. T. Masters for being the man that you are. I consider you to be a trophy worth more than any treasure ship I may have taken."

"Aaron, see to it that each of Mr. Heathman's scallywags are placed in separate closed in stable stalls with locked doors ad guarded by one of my warrior crewmen until I decide their fate. The scallywags appeared to be fearless. Each man did not know what the fate of the other would be."

My lieutenant kept one of the five henchmen tied to a rail at the barn. The other four rascals were placed in an individual horse stall at the stable. I am sure they thought the man we were keeping would be hung or worse. My instructions were to, after the other men were in the stalls, strip down the criminal that we had tied to the barn and put him on the road back to the place from which he left. The four men that were placed in the stalls were stripped of their clothing. The clothes were given to the guards. They could keep only their pants. I looked to Aaron and said, "I am sure they now think they are going to be executed."

I said, "Every four hours, I want you to gag one savage, take him to the road and send him off to go back from whence he came. Every four hours to the fifth man. There should be no meeting up with each other. I cannot see doing physical harm to any of them for they have not caused any physical harm to any of us. But, because of their expected intent in supporting Heathman, they need to be punished in this fashion...sans clothes and shoeless and walk back to London."

I said, "While my lieutenant is out purchasing the merchant ship, Aaron, you and I are going out fishing for bottles of whiskey and rum that may be on the Bounty." Aaron's wife, Ida Lee, and his two children were so happy that I cannot express how they looked and felt.

Our trip to the Bounty was a sorrowful one since we would not ever see the Bounty again. It would be our last trip to what was left of our old friend the Bounty. I said, "Aaron, the Bounty is where you and your parents started their business in England and provided you your needs and happiness and all the seamen that have spent their money there as well. That is where I met Annabelle and her many, many friends. Aaron, if I were not an officer, I believe I could have sobbed a little too when the Bounty burned."

But what a discovery we made. Though the cases of Irish whiskey and rum burned the bottles did not. There were multitudes of bottles that could not easily be counted as they bobbed around on the watery deck floor. They were floating absolutely everywhere. The passersby knew they did not dare to set foot onto that ship. They were right, for Aaron or his friends would have knocked a few heads together for those attempting to loot the property.

I said, "Aaron we are going to need boxes for this whiskey and rum and a wagon to haul it in." He said, "Yes Sir, Captain!" and left the ship. It was just minutes before he brought back to the ship his friends from the entertainment cast of the Bounty. I gave Aaron money and told him to buy a large wagon and more boxes which we will need to load up the remaining bottles of whiskey and rum.

At that time, I told everyone to stop loading the boxes and gather around. "I am going to tell you of a great opportunity in Cuba for you to make a new life for yourselves there. You will be hired at the Cuban casino to do the very thing you have been doing here on the Bounty and good news! Annabelle is managing that casino and will manage you there as she did here. So, pass the word to your fellow entertainers. You will be departing Friday at dawn. Be there! There will be no waiting and do not tell a soul except your family. If you have family bring them too, but do not tell anyone that you are leaving and I mean NO ONE or you will totally disrupt the plan."

Aaron arrived with wagons and boxes. Everything was loaded and moved to my ship the Annabelle, which was docked. I asked myself where will I put all this whiskey and rum. What a problem to have! There was not a room or place on board where I did not have those boxes of rum and whiskey stored. Much I had loaded on the merchant ship in care of Aaron's family and his horses were loaded as well. Do horses drink whiskey?!!

Aaron and I returned to his barn where Heathman and his colleague were sitting by the barn looking for help. He had been waving his hat in the air to signal his ruffians to attack.

"What are you doing Heathman? Waving away the fleas and gnats?!! He said, "Yes indeed I am Sir." I said, "I have taken care of that Heathman! They are not coming---now or ever! You must worry and wait for your fate. I told Aaron that maybe we should write a letter of confession for Heathman to sign for what he had done in burning the O'Hara's pub and threatening the life of Aaron's family. Just to get his beloved horse 'Royal Best' and Aaron's 'Trustworthy' back under his ownership."

Heathman has recognized his folly and decided to get a new start and go to Cuba on Captain Worthy's Warship. Our confessional letter carrier will be Heathman's brother, Darryl, who has sat by him the entire time. We have told Darryl it would be wise for his longevity to carry this message to the English lawman. I took this written confession to the barn where Heathman was mumbling and trembling and sweating as to what his fate might be. I pulled my sword and rested it by my side and held the confession in front of Heathman's face and said, "Read it and sign it!" I picked up the signed confession and put my epee back in its sheath and said, "Okay, for now!" and left. I wrapped this confession in sheepskin, tied it to Darryl's chest and saddled a horse. I helped Darryl straddle the horse and gave him the reins and said, "Ride and do not stop!"

I told Darryl Heathman that if he did not accomplish this order, I would soon know about it and I have many friends in London that would be happy for a few coins to bring his miserable life to an end.

I then slapped his horse on the rump. Darryl hung on for dear life and they sped out of sight on the road to London. I said, "Heathman, you are going to work for Aaron, the very man you threatened. I am going to let you keep your horse and carriage. They will be placed in the horses' area. You may have it as a shelter and a place to sleep. We will feed you the same food that we feed ourselves, but only after you feed and water the horses. It seems ironic, doesn't it, feeding and caring for the horses you coveted? From now on their care will be from you. Heathman you have plenty of blankets in your carriage to keep you warm on these cold nights at sea. Aaron take this mean man away. I don't want to see him again."

Mid-morning the next day my lieutenant arrived with a newly purchased merchant ship that had animal supplies and food supplies for Aaron's family. When that happened, the loading began. We made accommodations on the merchant ship, my warship and my escort ship. I knew not how many entertainers and their families might be coming along so I bought provisions for two hundred people. Many of them according to the accommodations each ship would have.

On Friday at dawn the entertainers and families that wanted to leave England arrived. The individual entertainers and those families amounted to one hundred twenty-five people. They were all assigned to their quarters as meager as they were. I sent word to all entertainers that life would be better than they ever had when they get to their new home in Cuba. I would personally see to it that that happened.

It was late afternoon before everyone was settled in and we could leave. About three p.m. on Friday we sailed away to Cuba.

I was pleased with myself that I managed to solve all problems, to my knowledge, without bloodshed.

What had started out to be just a mere visit to my brother-in-law had turned into a real crisis. Now I have a different kind of crisis.

I pride myself in my ability to plan well and foresee problems but guess what…I had forgotten land people cannot keep their food down because of motion sickness. I should have given the land people containers in which to puke…but I did not! They must have eaten well. Before long, as it turned out, there was an abundance of smelly stuff everywhere. Fortunately, much of it was coughed up over the rail of the ship. The fish were fed well during the next day or two of our journey. I demanded that they clean up their own mess and I then provided buckets of sea water, lye soap, and brushes to maintain some measure of respect to our warships and the men who have fallen to their death to the deck during the many battles and encounters with other warships.

I was resting in my room and musing over the decisions I had made during the last few days. I felt they were good ones. Then I suddenly heard both laughing and yelling and crying on the deck just outside my cabin.

I jumped from my bed, threw open my window and saw everyone looking at the sea around them. I thought, "My God, we are sailing amidst a pod of whales---adults and babies!" I yelled, "Quiet---be quiet!" They did not know why but they obliged me. You see, a huge whale with babies when tormented or frightened could charge upon a wooden ship. Their size and weight could bring a warship down especially when charged by several whales. I looked to the crow's nest and shook my fist at the seaman. He knew he should have spotted those whales easily. He knew he was facing one strike of the "cat".

We moved slowly through those many whales. The whales were spouting water and seemed very agitated. It was at least several hours that our three vessels treaded gingerly through the pod of whales. They could have destroyed our vessels as well as ourselves. I heaved a sigh of relief that I had evaded another life-and-death crisis.

Several hours later we left that problem and another enormous crisis lay before us. The man in the crow's nest screamed and pointed ahead as three Spanish Warships were bound toward us with intent to capture us! I suddenly felt an unusual sensation. It was fear because I felt responsible for the one hundred twenty-five Milford citizens and families aboard our three ships! I actually trembled because of that fear.

I was glad that I was the first of the two ships following me because I could attack oncoming ships head on! The merchant ship had no weapons, but my accompanying warship with my best Captain, quickly went to full sail to support me in my attack. I screamed, "Full sail!" Now my Annabelle sped through the waves head on towards the first ship. My expert cannoneers loaded my special long-range cannons at the bow. They aimed at the center masts of the on-coming warship. I said, "Wait…wait…now fire!" Those two cannoneers aimed with great precision!

The two cannoneers struck the base of the main mast on the lead warship. That mast went full forward and took out the front mast. They were disabled. I then steered the Annabelle to the left and positioned my starboard cannons just far enough away from the second Spanish galleon in order to place my cannon fire onto the deck and onto the gun side of the Spanish ship. The cannoneers swiftly fired the cannons at the waterline of the first ship which was crippled and started to sink. Captain John and I now looked to the second ship and brought down the warship. I fired my bow cannons and struck the deck of the second ship. Captain John brought his cannon fire to the starboard side while I spent my cannon fire towards its waterline. There were no risks to our ship. The second warship took on water and lost its mast and would soon sink. The third ship fled.

Now I have another problem…What to do with the two damaged Spanish galleons, and what to do with their crew? Many of their crew were injured. Those ships were mostly immobile and I could not accommodate three Spanish ships with all their seamen. Even if I could reach them, transferring people or anything from ship-to-ship on the high seas was a frightening and dangerous experience!

I did not have the right to expose my ship or Captain John's warship to try to rescue the enemy seamen. For the first time I decided not to help those Spanish ships. I sailed to the front of the merchant ship and Captain John took his place to the rear of the merchant ship and we sailed toward Cuba. I prayed that we would have no further combat. At that time, I wondered what happened to those two crippled ships and the crew that sailed them. To ease my mind, I hoped that the third Spanish ship that fled the scene would come back and rescue those crews or take the ships in tow back to Spain.

I am sure that our passengers would have much to talk about when we reached port in Cuba. Under full sail, I went to my cabin, sat in my chair, and thought through all that had happened since I had left England and Ireland to pay a visit to my brother-in-law.

I thank God for my specially made warship the Annabelle! I thank my great grandfather Captain Eric Worthy who had designed this great warship with all its special features and spent a good part of his fortune in having it built.

I realized that I was suddenly very sleepy and tired when just as soon as I started to sleep, there was a crash of thunder that awakened me. I threw on my raincoat and stepped out onto the deck just as more lightening flashed and more thunder roared. I prayed to God not to let the storm do us in!

Then it started---The waves were rolling the ship to and fro. Then larger waves started beating the hull and the wind was whistling through the sails. I felt our ship being tossed and turned in all directions. The heavy rains were crashing everything aboard the deck surface and sweeping away everything that was not tied down. My sails master and the crewmen were climbing the rope ladders to the yardarms to lower our sails. I could hear some sails ripping from the strong winds. I knew unless we could quickly drop those tall sails, we could be blown sideways and that our deck could take on so much water that it could turn us over on our side and the ship would sink and we would all drown. I could only see Captain John's Warship when the lightening glowed against its sails. His sails, too, were coming down. The merchant ship seemed stable. It was under light sail and that sail had been dropped. Now our ships were at the mercy of Mother Nature.

Our ships were just bobbing and being tossed up and down by the ever-changing direction of those mountains of waves. Never in all my days at sea have I seen or endured such a storm that I am now trying to survive.

There was no sleep that night. Thankfully the next morning the storm was over and the sea had subsided. I stood by the helm an watched the ships come alive again with all the seamen returning to their duties.

The sail master came to me and said, "We lost two men when they dropped into the sea as we dropped sails and another man was found this morning after he had fallen from the yardarm. He died when he hit the deck. I do not know Captain John's losses, if any, on his warship. But, for now, we will have a burial at sea and prayer for those who died." I said, "Absolutely!" Then we prepared for the ceremony.

Again, the men climbed the rope ladders and with the help of the winch they pulled the sails upward. Some sails that the waves ripped were useless.

In an hour we had our burial at sea and prayers for those who had died after dropping into the sea during the storm. I have had crew that felt depressed before but somehow this was different. I signaled Captain John to come closer to the ship so I could call to him. After doing so I said, "Captain did you lose anyone?" He said, "No Sir, thankfully not a one, but I do have many sick passengers." I said, "Tell your crew and passengers they may all have two rations of rum in celebration of weathering the storm. They are entertainers and are able to hold their grog, but double their portion of food for today." I went back to my cabin again and felt that everyone would soon be mellowed out by the rum and could relax. I will try to sleep a little myself.

I awakened when hearing a rapping at my cabin door. "Come in!" My second lieutenant said, "I believe we are getting near land sir. Would you be wanting to go to the helm of your ship sir as we enter the Cuban waters?" I said, "Yes I would! I am on my way!" After washing and shaving the whiskers from my chin, I dressed in my best captain's uniform. With my spy glasses, I looked to sea to see if one of my warships was protecting the harbor. It was not there. I said, "Lieutenant Perry, there is something wrong. My captains never disobey my orders. Lower us to half sail lieutenant and proceed to enter the harbor." I requested that all captains join me on the Annabelle. Soon four captains were seated in my cabin. I looked at them all squarely in their eyes and asked, "Why?"

Captain Beasley said, "We all received written orders from President Madarrga to anchor in the harbor and greet you for your homecoming." I said, "Captains, shame on you! Do you believe the Cuban President has precedence over my orders to you? Sirs, do you believe you have done wrong?" Each captain in turn said, "Aye!" I said, "Consider yourselves reprimanded with this disobedience. It will be noted in your record of service. Each of you sitting at this table have a ration of rum while I speak to you about what is happening and what we should do about it!" I said, "First, I believe Spain is planning to take control again of this island which is called 'Little Spain'. On our way back to Cuba, Captain John's Warship and my own Annabelle met three Spanish Warships. Just by estimating their direction there is no question that they were returning from Cuba or the Dominican Republic. I believe it was Cuba. Is that true captains? They each said, "Aye, Sir". I asked, "Why did you allow those three ships to enter the harbor?"

"Sir, we only allowed one to come to shore because it was bearing a peace flag. He merely wanted to speak to our President and then leave. He did so, within a few hours of meeting with the President. We couldn't sink his ship and kill his crew without real cause. The other Spanish Warships were anchored far from the harbor and we feel that they were just escort ships. It was not clear that you wanted us to have a war with every Spanish ship that moored on shore."

I said, "Captain, I see your dilemma. It is truly my fault. You were right in not engaging them as they seemed to be of no threat and did not give any indication that they wanted to pursue battle. You were right. We will put that aside for now. Gentlemen, I will give you a brief idea of what Captain John's Warship and my Warship have been through on the crossing of the sea!! Have a ration of rum and sit down and hear me out."

"We disabled two of the Spanish Warships and the third sailed away. We left those two warships some nautical miles from here---crew and all. I did not have the chance to interrogate either Captain of those two disabled ships. I suspect they left Spanish soldiers and I believe they off-loaded at least two hundred Spanish solders. It is possible that they had a fourth ship enter into port on the opposite side of Cuba, probably to take back Cuba.

Our three ships are carrying One hundred twenty-five entertainers who wanted to come to Cuba. They lost their livelihoods when the famous Bounty pub burned down. We must, in a few days, allow them to set foot on the Cuban shore and allow the livestock, including twelve thoroughbred champion horses, to be off-loaded somewhere along the harbor front where they can feed on grass. My intended plan is totally based on what I thought to be an invasion of Spanish ships on this Cuban harbor and its shore. Based on that belief, I want Captain Beasley and Captain Belford to race under full sail to those two Spanish ships that we disabled and abandoned. You must face them to the front to avoid any thoughts they may have of using their cannons to bring you down. I need one brave volunteer to go to the enemy ship and tell the captains to run up the white flag and bring all of their crewmen and cannoneers to the rail of the ships so that by spyglass we can see them all. Unless they acknowledge defeat by the white flag, we will sink their ships and everyone will drown. Two ships will be deployed in order to accomplish this task. Tell the enemy captains to acknowledge immediately. Now Captains Beasley and Belford, be off with you. Bring at least one captain back alive. Use your fifty warrior crewmen from both ships to board the enemy ships.

Place the captains on Captain Beasley's ship and put the ships' officers in their own brig. Lower all sails on both the enemy ships. Attach long docking ropes to the ship's bow in any way you can and pull those ships back one hundred yards off shore. Then anchor them facing west. We will use their two hundred forty cannons against any enemy ships headed this way into Cuban waters."

After the enemy ships were anchored off shore, I asked that my lieutenants, if any of them wished to, station themselves on each of the anchored enemy ships that were captured and conduct cannon fire on any of the enemy ships. There were just enough sails hanging from their yardarms to slowly maneuver these ships into position outside the harbor and the lieutenants were able to help do this.

After positioning these enemy ships, place your ships one hundred yards on either side of the disabled Spanish enemy ships, but leave enough passage to the port for my own ship to pass through. Now, the two captains remaining---Captain John and Skinner---place your ships in lie with the other ships facing west.

We were in line and there would be six ships aligned facing west to meet the Spanish ships that would be heading our way. Before you take your position in line, one of you please start taking the passengers on Captain John's ship and my ship and move them to the merchant ship, and tell them to take provisions with them. I will take my merchant ship to the inlet near the harbor entry where the water is deep. I will pull the merchant ship close to shore and let the passengers disembark, along with Aaron's twelve thoroughbred horses, or they may stay on board the merchant ship for the protection from weather and for food provisions.

I said, "Captain John, I want the best of your fifty warrior crewmen to find their way to the docking area of the palace. For the captain of the Neptune, I want your fifty warrior seamen to enter the docking area east of the palace. I want each of your warrior seamen to individually and gradually take position on each side closest to the palace. Do not act like you are going to fight or invade the palace. When you hear Captain John and I beat a drum, it will be same drum sound you would hear when someone is walking the plank. When you hear sounds of the drum from our ship, walk as if you are a friend and at the first opportunity stab the soldier in the throat so he cannot yell. If you are unsure about the men who once worked for me then say, "Friend or Foe". I believe you will find the men I placed as their palace guards still have allegiance to myself. They may have been coerced into taking a palace guard position.

Kill all soldiers in the Spanish military quietly with a dagger to the throat. All other guardsmen just say the word – "Captain Worthy". If they are suddenly defiant, stab them. If they are friends, let them live and have them join in confronting the next guardsmen. Do the same with every guardsman throughout the palace. I expect that there will be no fewer than one hundred soldiers in uniform surrounding the president's palace. As soon as you have completed your mission, come to me where I will have the Annabelle docked in front of the palace. I want you warriors to slowly climb the steps and go into every room and enter and tie up the civilians and stab the soldiers. I do not know how long that will take, but I want a few of your best fighters to go directly through the double doors where you will find the President's office. Dismiss any guard outside the President's office. As soon as you hear the word "come", swiftly enter the room, pistols loaded and swords ready to fight the soldiers that I believe are guarding him. Do not enter until I say "come". I thought to myself, when I enter, I will know then if I made a terrible mistake. If I don't see the President, I will know I was right.

It was not long before I found my way to the President's office door. Outside in an official tone I had my men say "Captain Worthy is here per your order Mr. President."

He called, "Good, by all means let him in!" I entered the office. I was terrified because there stood Annabelle on the side of the imposter. He said, "You're looking for your president, are you?"

"Yes, I am," I said. The imposter said, "The Spanish officials promoted him to a Viceroy in Mexico. Two days ago, he left with his family and belongings to Mexico and took his new position as Viceroy. I am substituting for the President until the new Governor arrives within a few days." I said, "Whoever you are, why do you have my wife with you?"

"To be honest Captain Worthy, I am taking your Annabelle hostage to be sure that the transfer of power to Spain is made without objection. You will see a small armada of Spanish ships arrive soon at the harbor. One ship will carry the dignitaries and the warship will do battle as necessary. Don't worry your family will be safe as long as you do hot attack my person or any of my entourage. Since you have been such an obedient Captain, I will allow you to join a Spanish fleet, maintain your home and keep some of your money or you and all of your family will be placed on a merchant ship with other defiant ones and sent east back to England."

I responded, "Mr. Governor, won't you at least let me hug my wife since I have been gone so long?" He said, "Yes, I will." At that moment I yelled out as if it was to Annabelle, "come!". Then Annabelle came dashing towards me. That was the signal for my warriors to burst into the room. Fighting ensued with all those in the room. I drew my pistol and shot the Governor between the eyes. It was over in minutes.

There were at least a dozen soldiers laying about. Many were dead. I lost one young crewman and two were injured. I was also injured. I received a gash on my rump, but it beats the hell out of being dead. Saving my family was worth it!

I will have to sleep on my stomach or left side for a while until the stitches mend both on my bottom and my pants. My bottom hurts but it was barely skin deep. I bled like a stuck pig. I moved slowly to the palace window and waved to the many crewmen and others who were standing by my ship the Annabelle. They applauded. They did not know a big sea battle was yet to come. There will be injury and death.

Annabelle and I went to her parent's home and I spent the afternoon telling them all the things that had happened since we left. They were: the burning of the Bounty, the death threats over a horse race, sailing through the pod of whales, the worst storm I have ever experienced, and the battle with the three Spanish ships.

I want my family to know that my son was with me through all these experiences except during the sea battles. During the battles, I made him stay in my armor- plated ship's cabin. You must know the greatest crisis of all is about to happen. I have placed my four warships and two captured ships in line one hundred fifty meters out of the eastern shore. I faced all cannons eastward.

Captain Beasley had found out from one of the enemy warships that we disabled, that there was an armada of sixteen Spanish warships on their way to invade Cuba and take back what they call "Little Spain". I believe they may arrive in just a day or two. We sat there in quiet and prayed that we would win this battle. Things were quiet as we sat there in awe and wonderment of all the things that were happening. I said, "Mickey, your son cam back with us. You will be seeing him tomorrow. He is currently finding shelter for his thoroughbred horses which we brought back on a merchant ship along with the one hundred twenty-five entertainers from the Bounty and their families. I had not told you this. You must be thrilled to know there will be only four of you again."

Annabelle squealed with glee and danced in circles at his good fortune. "I will have real and true friends again!", she said.

Again, quiet prevailed. It was so quiet you could hear over your heart beat. In breaking the silence, there was a rapping at the O'Hara's door. Mickey went to his door, opened it and saw a very tall, thin man. He was nearly as tall as the Captain. Mickey asked, "What do you want?" The thin man replied, "Just to meet you, Sir!" I said, "Mickey and Anne, I invited Booker T. T. Masters to visit you. Our plan is for him to be our new school master in a school I will build for him." Mickey said, "Joseph, just what does this tall, thin man know that we don't?" Go ahead Mr. Booker T. T. Masters, give me a list of the skills you wish to teach. The thin man said, "Mr. O'Hara, I am proficient in Spanish, French, German and Italian. I am also proficient in writing, reading and speaking them. I speak some Danish and can talk to you in simple Gaelic if you choose." Mickey spoke a few words of Gaelic to the thin man and the thin man responded. Mickey was as happy as if he had just received a case of Irish Whiskey.

The thin man said, "Sir, I am also well versed in numbers which is called mathematics. These things I will teach the teachers to teach. You will be pleased to know I am a master in using the pistol and epee. You will now see your grandson Will, Mr. O'Hara, for he will be with me during every class I teach."

Then Mickey piped up and said, "I would like to see at least one of the skills you can demonstrate right here in my home." I said, "Mickey, I must tell you that it is true that he has bested me in the use of the epee, for he learned from a French master. He has hit the bucket target with his pistol shot, "dead on" from thirty paces away. He did not say, but he has attended a chef school in France. He would probably like to demonstrate those skills here if Anne chooses. Anne, I am sure you can teach him a thing or two about Irish cooking." Mr. Booker T.T. Masters said, "Yes, Mrs. O'Hara, I would be so happy if you so choose!"

I said, "Mr. Thin Man has not told me of his other skills." The thin man said, "Daggers and blades of all kinds!"

Mickey said, "I am placing this King of Hearts playing card one-third of the way down inside my front door. Now, Mr. Thin Man, step twenty meters away from that card and I will lend you that dagger to see how close you can come." The thin man stepped twenty meters away from that very small King of Hearts target and took the dagger and without hesitation, threw it and hit the head of the King of Hearts. We all applauded. Mickey applauded the most of all and he said, "Never have I seen the like. Show me once again Mr. Thin Man!" Mickey handed the thin man his throwing blade and said, "Show me again!"

The thin man cocked his arm back and threw that blade directly and so fast that you could barely see it in mid-air. It penetrated the King of Hearts playing card directly into the heart of the King.

Mickey screamed, "Never have I seen it! Never thought it could be done! Twice in a row!" Everyone applauded and Mickey said, "You are a master-in-arms and I want to give you two things that I cherish." Mickey then went to his little treasure chest and brought forth a dagger and a throwing blade. Mickey said, "Mr. Masters, honor me by accepting this ivory handled, silver plated dagger that you may strap on your boot. I also wish to present to you this ivory handled gold plated throwing knife for you to strap anywhere on your body as well."

I believe that Booker T. T. Masters was a perfect name for a school master and also a master-at-arms. The thin man looked down at Mickey and said, "It would be an honor to accept such fine weapons as these. I will always remember you when I look at them. I am leaving now Mr. and Mrs. O'Hara, but before I leave, I promise you, my captain, I will break my rule to not use weapons and kill. I wish to be at your side with your lieutenants during all of your sea battles. I want to protect you as you have protected me."

Mickey said, "Wait, Mr. Masters, I want you to return soon to give me ideas on this new invention of mine. It is to be a folding blade about four or five inches in length. A blade that can be folded back into its case and kept in your pocket. I will call it a pocket knife. I would appreciate any ideas you may have to contribute to my invention." Mr. Masters then said, "Happily, I will do so!" He then turned swiftly, opened the door and left. We all ran to the front window to see him leave in his new carriage. It was a sight to behold as we saw Mr. Masters skip to his carriage. I called to him at the door, "Thin man, teach that to the children." I think I embarrassed him. He called back, "Bye, see you soon." I had noticed that soon after his visit to the O'Hara's the children were skipping here and there, and they have added a hop and a jump to a new game that they called hopscotch. It should be called "Hop Irish"!

It is also time for me to leave. I told my family "Do not worry. I often turn a negative into a positive." I then gave Anne O'Hara a kiss on her forehead and a small hug and then picked up my "big boy" Will and we gave each other mutual hugs---No kisses! I reached for Mickey's hand, and he said, "Captain Joseph, I think of you as a son and love you as such. I want a hug too, and indeed I gave him a huge, long bear hug that turned him a little red in the face. I grabbed Annabelle's hand. We went out the front door and I looked into her teary eyes and they sparkled all the more. I ran my fingers through her red hair and gave her little kisses all over her face and then our lips met in one long sweet kiss. I gently pressed her head slightly backward, so I could look directly down into that beautiful Irish face. I wanted to imprint into my mind the image of that lovely face, so later I could see her through my mind's eye. I stroked her cheeks once more. I kissed her palms and released her dainty hands and turned and walked slowly down the pathway. I choked back that feeling of wanting to sob and resisted. But I could not resist the tears that filled my eyes. I used the heel of my palm to wipe away the tears that kept coming, and I finally stood by my borrowed horse that I got from my brother-in-law.

I stood there with my face against the neck of my borrowed horse until I could see clearly without tears blocking my vision. I placed my right foot on the ground and with a slight jump I straddled my mount. I gave it a slight bump on its flank, rattled the rein and it sped off. That horse thought it was in some kind of a race and I had to try to slow it down. I headed off to where I was scheduled to meet with my captains for further planning of our war with the Spanish armada.

My crew was present as well as the warrior crewmen and officers. I asked, "Have you brought me the best cannoneers of all that we have?" Captain John said, "We have sir!" I began, "Now would you please remove every item on the Annabelle to the dock unless it is nailed down or screwed in place. I mean beds and everyone's belongings. I want to reduce the weight of the Annabelle to its minimum. As you know our ship is specially made with a narrow beam and special sails and cannons so it can move swiftly on the sea. With the reduction of weight, I can go faster. Now, with this additional speed I am going to circumvent the Spanish armada warships. I am going to attack those warships from the rear, one at a time. Because my cannons are of long range, I can hit their ships and they cannot hit mine. I will disable as many as I can from the rear and continue to maintain my distance so their cannon fire cannot reach us.

My captains then left the meeting to take over the upcoming battles. I will continue to bring down as many of these Spanish warships as possible as soon as they come into bear. Good luck to you all. Be sure there is plenty of cannon ball powder and that each cannon has enough fire to put down a half dozen ships. Do not spend all of your cannon fire on one ship. I saw that my cannoneers and officers were headed to the storehouse to get more gun powder, cannon balls, and wadding for our cannons. I told my two cannoneers at the Annabelle to do the same and get a lot of cannon balls and powder. It took nearly two hours before everyone was in place and on board and we could untie our mooring line under "soft sail".

We sailed our way to the front line of our six ships that were anchored. I ordered full sail. We adjusted sails and our rudder to travel north by north west for two miles. Then I changed directions to the east. With my spy glasses I could discern those Spanish ships a mile to the south. I then took the helm and gently made a u-turn to the north and then to the east.

So far, I am exactly where I want to be. I sped under full sail. I moved closer to the warships. I said, "Use the cannon fire in two of your ships to the right at the first single ship that comes into sight. On the left side of your line, you will do the same. The middle two ships on our line will do the exact same thing to the first ship they have on sight. Just think of it as being two on one and keep up that process.

The other cannoneers make ready, for we might use you in future battles. You seamen handling the sails are among the best for you will need to be because I will be ordering you to adjust sails and make quick turns.

Bow cannoneers get ready to blast at the masts of the enemy ship just ahead on three...one...two...three!! I want each of my bow cannoneers to receive assistance in front loading. Therefore, four more cannoneers are needed to assist. The cannoneers let forth a volley with the long guns. The aim was on target. It hit the bottom of the main mast on the trailing ship. The main mast fell backwards. It took out and brought down the other two masts. We cheered and then moved just out of range of their cannons to the North. I said, "All cannoneers on both decks fire at the water line of that trailing ship. On Three! Fire!" They fired all at once. All eighty cannons from both decks were fired. The blast shook the Annabelle. The volley of cannonballs hit the waterline of that warship and it began taking on water.

The cannons on one side of the enemy ship were pointing down and the other cannons on the other side of the ship were pointing skyward.

No cannons could do any damage. Soon it would sink…it was totally disabled.

I then sailed to their next warship and my bow cannoneers with their two long cannons together hit the ship directly on its center mast with the cannonballs. The mast fell towards the front taking along the other masts. I sailed Annabelle near the injured ships. My cannoneers on the port side reloaded and they sent a volley of cannonballs to the waterline of that enemy ship. You could see the ship open and take in water. It immediately listed to the North and was quickly sinking. The next two ships turned to protect themselves and avenger their losses. With the swiftness of our ship we easily assumed a position where their cannonballs couldn't reach us…though they tried. Our cannons had been reloaded and we fired all forty cannons on the broadside of the waterline of their ship. They hit the target and again their cannons, due to the listing of the ship, were pointed downward and again some of their cannons were pointed upward so all of them were ineffective. So far, we put down three warships.

The fourth warship had no possibility of out-maneuvering us as the Annabelle swiftly maneuvered herself to place another volley of cannonballs to the waterline of that fourth ship. I am proud because I am the only ship sinking the enemy. I alone with my crew are gradually defeating the enemy from the rear. I will continue sinking enemy ships as best as I can until I no longer have cannonballs or powder. Then I will circumvent those enemy ships and since I have no more fodder for my cannons, I must sail my ships back to the harbor and resupply my cannonballs and barrels of powder. I now have disabled four of their trailing warships. I wondered how many more ships there were because now they had spread out in both direction—North and South---but still in line towards Cuba. Our ships were waiting for them and they were fully loaded and ready to sink as many Spanish ships as possible. The best I could tell is that there were still twelve Spanish warships that were untouched and were bearing down on Cuba. Soon after being loaded with firepower, I sped out of the harbor and again circumvented the oncoming ships to bring my long cannons ripping through every ship's mast I could see. Very soon the cannon fire from all of my eight warships at anchor were hitting their targets on the enemies' front line of ships. At one time when all the cannons went off at once there were probably four hundred cannonballs in the air dropping down on the Spanish armada. Let it be known that the one ship with the dignitaries was not shot at. You would know it by the special flags that were hoisted atop all masts.

It was about two hours later when I sailed past my line of warships that I noticed a previously damaged ship was sinking. I never considered it to be one of mine. Many of my men, however, felt the sting of firepower. As I sailed by each Captain, they signaled to me if they had lost any men and if they died, he would pump his arms up and down to indicate how many. Every ship on line had lost a few good seamen and I lost two of my beloved lieutenants on those previously captured ships that were anchored in the center of my line of ships. The enemy ships that were sunk or disabled lost many men. These men were injured or dying or drowning men who were dying due to a large sea battle. You could hear them screaming for help. They were injured or dying. It was eerily quiet.

Captain John escorted the Spanish ship with the dignitaries to the harbor port and to the mooring place at the dock. At gunpoint they were ordered to remain on their ship until I arrived. After I moored o the dock, my captains accompanied me to that "so called" dignitary ship. The ship was secured to the dock as well as an off-board plank. It was a beautiful ship, just like the Bounty that had been burned down in England. This ship will now belong to the O'Hara's who owned the Bounty. Here he came strutting down the ramp as if he was a kind of God.

You could tell he was one of his King's favorites. He was dressed in finery that I cannot fully describe. There were four handsomely dressed men that accompanied him. We met face-to-face and I said, "Why can't you leave Cuba alone? Why did you cause this war and cause the deaths of so many of your men? Your ships and fellow countrymen are either drowning or dead. What is your name Sir?"

He said, "I was appointed to be the new Governor of Cuba. My name is Juan Fransisco de Guemes. Cuba has always been our 'Little Spain' and provided us with their exports that we dearly need. They have our culture, our religion, and our language and will always be of Spanish descent."

I said, "Mr. Guemes, we have made the people of your 'Little Spain' independent and happy. Talk to any citizen and they will tell you that they do not want to be living under the control and laws of Spain. I will personally escort you to a carriage and go to all parts of Cuba. They will tell you how they have sufficient wealth to survive and continue to be happy. You see Governor, we ask the going market price for everything England buys from Cuba. England and all other countries are required to treat Cuba as a separate country with its own constitution and its own President.

We have done away with the imposter and crew that was trying to take over Cuba. They are all dead. All of the one hundred soldiers that you sent here to assist in that cause have been killed. It is just you and your associates that remain directly connected to King Ferdinand. All of the others are dead.

Governor De Guemes, you, your wife and four of your associates, along with my wife and I will escort you throughout Cuba. You and your wife and my wife and I will be in one carriage and your four associates will ride in a second carriage for the tour. You will not want a change. The Cubans pay their fair share of taxes based on their income. The Cuban Casino and all the businesses pay taxes according to the profits they make. As a result, they now have better roads, better gas lighting, better sewer systems, more and clearer water wells, and more smoke houses to protect the fish from spoiling. They grow more tobacco and make more cigars. The tourists love to visit here for there are more jails to maintain the law and order.

Before I came this was a poor country with sad people, but now that I have built more hospitals to care for people and brought in more doctors, there are fewer deaths. I have built more schools for more students who wish to learn a trade. Instead of wanting to take over and bleed this country and give them nothing in return, your King should instead be building a good, healthy relationship with the people who now live happily in this separate island called Cuba!"

I was so happy to see that this now proposed Governor believed that what I had said to them was true. At the end of our excursion, the "want-to-be" Governor de Guemes told me that everything that he had heard from King Ferdinand of Spain was wrong. The new Governor said, "I have seen the power that you have in protecting Cuba. If you would permit me, I would love to be Governor and continue all the good things that you have started. I will pledge allegiance to England and you to do the best that I am able to perpetuate all the good things that you have done or have started to happen. I will sign any document that England or you may have to officially give me this authority." I said, "Governor, I will support you and see to it that you are proclaimed to be Governor of this country which you may now call a Republic."

I told the Governor, "I will see to it that no foreign power will be allowed to come to your palace and intimidate or coerce you into leaving your position as this country's leader! God bless you, Governor! You have beautiful quarters and wonderful office space from which you can to your bidding. Remember this---I will not take orders from you in any way, but will do those things to support any and all fair requests that you make."

Annabelle and I bowed to them and we went to our pretty cottage on the cove. Annabelle and I and our family and all acquaintances have spent happy and prosperous years here. We really have no good reason to leave our happy home. It is wonderful to see Aaron and his family settle in on his acreage. It is fun to see how he is training his thoroughbreds and his entries into the Cuban races that the horsemen enjoy. My huge wealth that has been amassing in the bank is almost embarrassing. We see no one around that needs our financial help any more, so we do not offer it. I said "Annabelle are you happy?" Annabelle said, "I am fine Joseph, but I long for more adventures, don't you?" I said, "Oh my God, yes I do! Let's take that adventure again, shall we?" I heard her whisper, "Could we?" I said, "You bet we can!" Annabelle said, "I believe I've had my fill of singing, dancing and managing the entertainment at the Cuban casino. Gambling has changed. There are several Italians that are now taking over and contracting the gambling equipment. This is not the same as it was when I came. I will be happy to leave it! Even my entertainers are leaving and finding their own mates to establish new lives."

The next morning, I called my four warship captains to meet me at my home. By noon they had all arrived and Annabelle served everyone a large measure of rum. Of course, we invited Annabelle's parents--- Mickey and Anne and her brother Aaron. "Gentlemen" I said, "I could see the longing in your eyes that after this length of time you want to move on with new conquests and adventures. That is why I made you captains of my warships. Annabelle and I also wish to move on to new adventures. It's easy just to stay put and make these boring voyages around the islands. I fear that maybe you and your cannoneers and crew have become rusty. Therefore, before I make my suggestions, I want you to know that while I was in England drawing the balance of my wealth from the London Bank, and helping Aaron, I heard some disturbing information. I followed up and confirmed this information that England was amassing an armada and is coming westward to support its position in the American colonies. Many other ships were instructed to claim the Dominican Republic and the island south of America as part of the English Kingdom."

I continued, "I tell you as your commander that our ships bare English flags, and because we are English, we have nothing to fear except that the armada will expect and require that we rejoin the English Navy because we are part of the English Navy and paid by the them.

As your commander, my wife, Annabelle and I, will give up that pay easily and head our warship west to visit Puerto Rico, Jamaica and the other islands. We plan to travel up the Mississippi with our warship and buy a new steamboat or paddleship, as they call them, and head north. I have given all of you the opportunity to stay where you are and join the English armada or go your own way and settle where you choose. I know that I have seen to it that each of you have a small fortune to do with as you choose. If you choose not to accompany me, I am, at this moment, releasing you from my command and authority. Of course, I will put that in writing. In any fashion, whether I release you or not, I will give you my word to give you freedom to go anywhere that you choose. I will see to it that you are provided with a merchant ship of your own to transfer your property, your family, your friends and their family to anywhere you desire. This I offer you today! I expect sometime tomorrow each of you will come to me and tell me of your decision. I know this is a paramount change in your lives and your family will need to be with you on this decision. So tomorrow, knock at my door at any time and let me know what you so choose to do. In any case, we will be leaving this island after I explain to the good Cuban Governor the reasons why I must go!"

I have never seen my captains so distressed. It was, of course, a shock for the to hear the words I said to them. There was only Captain Beasley I was concerned for. He showed fear and anxiety for being left alone to make his decisions. He was like a son that needed his father near him.

The next day everyone's lives were about to change---or not! Mickey and Anne and Aaron were the first to arrive at our home. Annabelle was ready with sweet rolls and Irish coffee. Mickey confronted me first and said, "This is just like before when you left us in England. This time we are not staying behind as we did in England. We are joining you---you, Will and our daughter and hopefully Aaron."

I said, "That is admirable. I am very proud and pleased! You will have quarters in one of the three extra cabins we have on my warship." Aaron said, "I want to go with the family on this adventure and bring along my horses on the merchant ship you have acquired. Wherever I go I can sell or race any of my horses." I said, "Aaron, we will probably be settling in Mid-America as we go up the Mississippi and find the perfect place to settle and you too will again have your horse farm and barn and breed and sell horses to the pioneers at a very high price!" Aaron said, "Great, I cannot wait!"

Then there came a rapping at my door. I said, "Come in!" Mr. Booker T. T. Masters entered and said, "I wish to go with you commander! I wish to take part in this new adventure!" I said, "Mr. Tall Thin man I am proud you made that decision. I may need your expert protection on the way to where ever we settle. But, more than that, I will still have you to tutor my son, Will, and myself!"

Everyone had left my house now to tend to packing for the adventure. As usual Captain John would see to it that all ships are packed with food and water. With Aaron's help, they will be loading many bales of hay and containers of grain for the horses.

Annabelle and I smiled and Annabelle said, "Joseph, I am thrilled to once again go on this new adventure. After the years we have spent here in Cuba doing the same thing day after day the voyage will be exciting." I said, "Me too! So, start all of your packing as Aaron will soon be coming by with his hired helpers to start loading our belongings."

We wanted to find out what other captains were going to do. One-by-one, they came throughout the day. Captain John said, "Sir, I am with you where ever you go. I will be your escort with my crew. I have talked to my crew and they wish to be with you as I do." I said, "Thank you

Captain John. I am so happy and proud you are with me. I'll feel more comfortable with you and your warship by my side!" Captain John said, "I too will be preparing. My wife and I and my son will all prepare to make the voyage. He added, Please, let me know, Sir, when you wish to depart and like always, I'll be ready." Just as he left Caption Beasley arrived and said "My family and I have decided to stay right here, even though I'll miss your direction so very much, I may have to get that from the leader of our English Fleet and join them!"

I said, "You are an honest man. You have always been an honest man and I wish you the very best. Beasley said, "Thank you, Sir!", and nodded his head and then he left.

Soon Captain Skinner arrived and that happy, courageous Skinner looked me in my eyes and said, "Sir, with your permission I am going to venture on without your leadership. My family wishes to make a new home in either Puerto Rico or Jamaica. That is where you will find us!"

Captain Skinner left, but before he could get out the door, Captain Belford came in and gave me a big friendly grin. Belford was the one who gave us laughs at our meetings. He said, "Sir, Captain, I have never told you, but I have thought of you as a father and protector. But like a good son, I am leaving now to venture out on my own with my family. You have given me riches and the ability to make decisions. I have no idea where myself or my warship will be going. Isn't that part of the adventure?"

In so many ways, when I felt down, he made me feel good. Belford left immediately. I turned to my family and said, "Every captain has made his decision. Annabelle, I feel a heavy weight has been lifted from my shoulders, since I will not have the responsibility of commanding the warships."

Annabelle replied, "I can already see that you are more relaxed and content."

I said, "Annabelle, I must now report to Governor de Guemes and tell him of these changes. I'll return soon and help with the loading of the ships."

I ventured to the palace. I went directly to the Governor's office. I was welcomed inside. The Governor said, "Please join me for a good Cuban cigar and a glass of Irish Whiskey, for I already sense that you are about to tell me either good news or bad news." I said, "Yes, Governor". I sat and took a sip of whiskey and a good drag from that cigar and just rested for a bit. Neither one of us said anything. I finally said, "Governor, I am off to a new adventure! All of my captains have been released to go their own way. Except for Captain Beasley and his warship. They will remain with you and provide some protection. I am sure Spain will once again wish to include you as part of their country. I am sure they will have other plans for you, and other Governors will follow as they have in the past. Cuba has deep roots with your mother country of Spain and I expect that will not change. I hope that since Cuba is now strong again with businesses and agriculture that you will keep it that way. My Annabelle and I will take our adventures north up the Mississippi and settle into new fertile fields along the way."

The Governor said, "In many ways I wish I were you. I can only thank you for all the fortune you have spent in building our country again with new businesses, hospitals, schools and increasing the silver that we are mining and minting. Please take your fortune from the bank. With the continued income for taxes and the casino, I will have ample wealth to continue those things you have started." The Governor put down his cigar and drink as I did mine, and he came to me and gave me a big hug and a handshake. He said, "Goodbye Captain Worthy and take that box of Cuban cigars with you and have a great voyage."

It wasn't long before I arrived to assist Annabelle and the rest of the crew in loading our belongings. I went to the bank and with the help of two of my crewmen, I loaded a wagon with the coin I had minted from the silver and gold bars. They will spend more easily. How do you spend a bar of gold or silver!? We transferred that huge fortune and distributed it on my ship, Captain John's warship and the merchant ship. There was so much coin that it actually changed the position of the height of the water line on all three vessels! I left the paper money. It was money of the French, English, German and Spanish. This money I designated to be spent at the hospitals and schools.

It was a very fair Sunday morning. Everyone and their families and Aaron's horses were loaded on the ships. Captain John especially was ready with his belongings aboard the ship.

EPILOGUE

My readers, there is so much more that I know will come in time as we tour the islands. I will bring to you another report of our adventures. So please, when you see a second sequel to this long adventure, GIVE IT A READ! Thank you for getting to know us and accompany us. It is not really the end. I am sure there will be confrontations with other cultures and Indians and pioneers. There will be harrowing experiences for Aaron and his thoroughbred horses. There will be challenges with traders and looters attempting to steal and harass. We will be coming in contact with outlaws and lawmen, and you will be amazed at the paradise that we find and how we settle it and what our goals were in creating a wild bird sanctuary. Also, how we assisted people in building their businesses around the beautiful lakes and our sanctuary. You will meet some really fun and interesting characters!

This time I will be building a small city around these small lakes and the folks we will be working with will be of all nations, but primarily English, French and German. You will hear a lot more about Will, my son, in the new book. Until now he has spent most of his time with the thin man who has become his second father, his protector and his friend.

Commander Joseph Worthy

Annabelle, my wife

And Annabelle, our warship

Printed in the United States
By Bookmasters